For Alys and her Mum . . . Always – M.S.

For George and Charlie – A.B.

Bloomsbury Publishing, London, Oxford, New York, New Delhi and Sydney

First published in Great Britain in 2017
by Bloomsbury Publishing Plc
50 Bedford Square, London WC1B 3DP

www.bloomsbury.com

BLOOMSBURY is a registered trademark of Bloomsbury Publishing Plc

Text copyright © Mark Sperring 2017
Illustrations copyright © Alison Brown 2017

A CIP catalogue record of this book is available from the British Library

ISBN 978 1 4088 7332 8 (HB)
ISBN 978 1 4088 7333 5 (PB)
ISBN 978 1 4088 7331 1 (eBook)

All papers used by Bloomsbury Publishing are natural, recyclable products made
from wood grown in well managed forests. The manufacturing processes
conform to the environmental regulations of the country of origin

Printed in China by Leo Paper Products, Heshan, Guangdong

1 3 5 7 9 10 8 6 4 2

I'll Love You Always

Mark Sperring
&
Alison Brown

BLOOMSBURY

LONDON OXFORD NEW YORK NEW DELHI SYDNEY

How long will I love you?
A second is too short.
A second is no time
for a love of this sort.

A minute is no better, for minutes fly by!

They're gone in a moment like a sweet butterfly.

An hour's still nothing –
it whirls by so fast.

I'll love you much longer than hours can last.

A morning is so brief,
an afternoon, too.

From sunrise to sunset,
I'll keep loving you.

Will I love you when night falls?

Of course, and beyond . . .

Will I love you tomorrow?
Oh yes, on and on . . .

I'll love you for whole days
stretched out in a line.

I'll love you for weeks
and a much longer time!

I'll love you for months
heaped up to the sky.

I'll love you through seasons
as they bluster by.

I'll love you for whole years
and though things might change . . .
as you grow bigger
my love stays the same.

How long will I love you?
If you need to know,
I'll tuck you in tightly,
then whisper it low . . .

I'll love you for years and for
months, weeks and days.
I'll love you for hours
and minutes

. . . always.

I'll love you forever, not one second less.
For that is what mummies and daddies do best.